Team Up with Batman!

adapted by J. E. Bright

based on the episode, "Night of the Batmen!"
teleplay by Paul Giacoppo

Batman created by Bob Kane

Reader's Digest
Children's Books®

New York, New York • Montréal, Québec • Bath, United Kingdom

Space pirate Kanjar Ro wants to attack an alien planet! It is up to Batman and his friends to save the day! Working with Batman, Aquaman and Green Arrow hold off Kanjar Ro's robots. Shazam and Martian Manhunter attack the pirate's ship while Batman gets to work on the bomb headed for the planet.

But wait . . . Batman can't disarm the bomb . . . and it is going to explode in seconds!

OH NO!

0:34

5

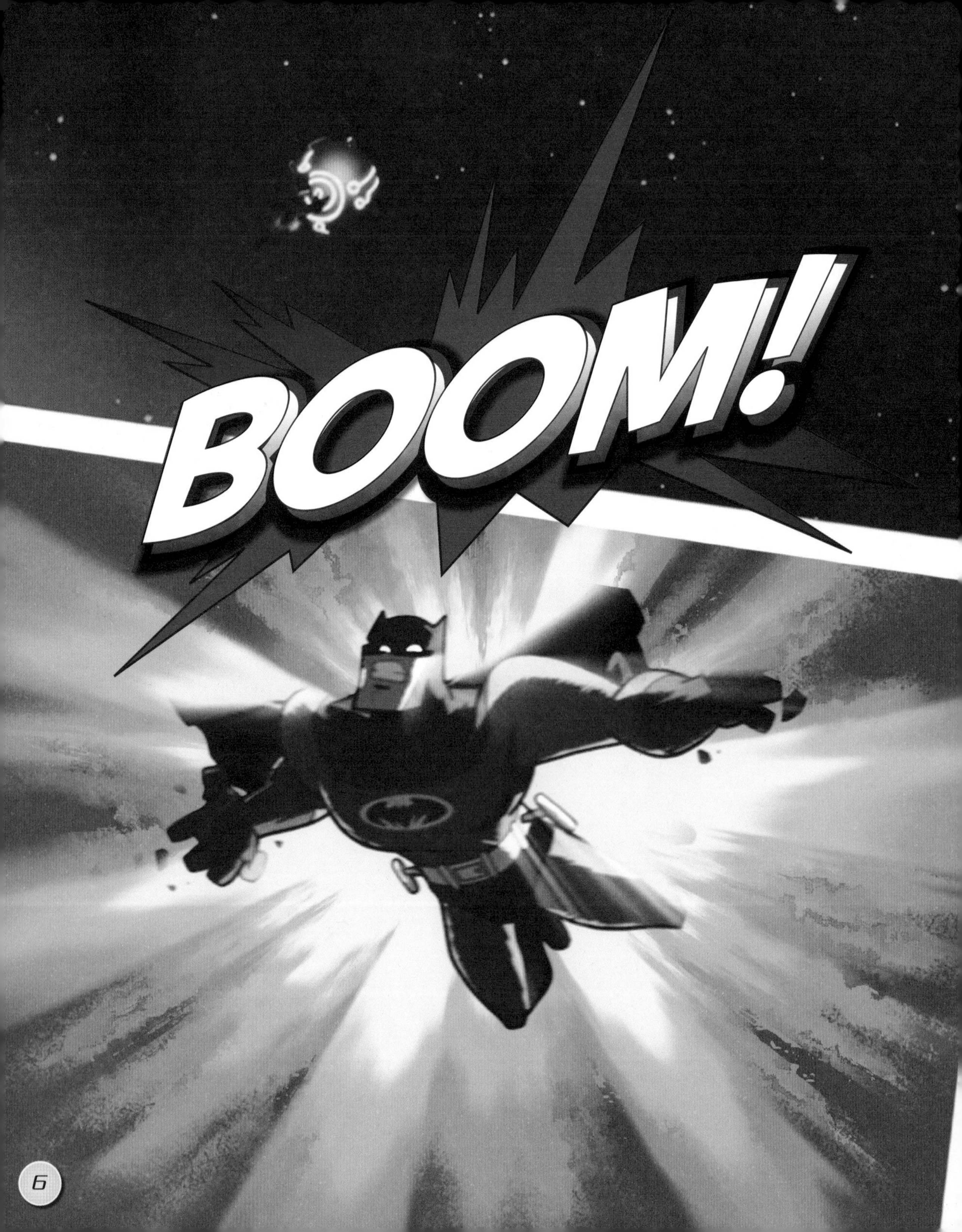
BOOM!

Batman pushes the bomb into outer space. Then. . .
BOOM! His quick thinking saves the alien world, but he is
injured by the explosion.
Batman's friends rush him home to safety.

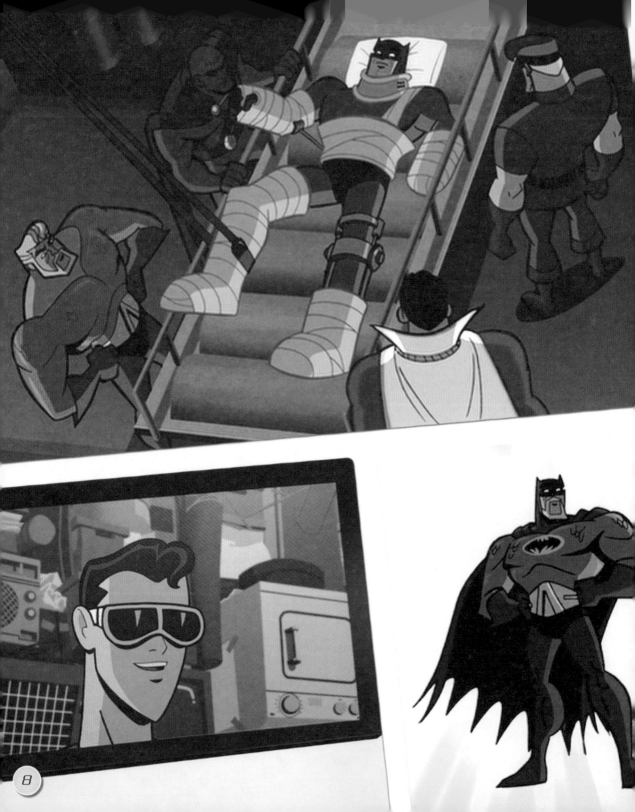

Batman wakes in Martian Manhunter's space station. He has been badly injured and will be bedridden for weeks. "But Gotham City needs me!" argues Batman. Everyone promises to keep Batman's injuries a secret. But Plastic Man, Green Arrow, Aquaman, and Shazam make plans of their own. Secretly, they each decide to handle Batman's duties until he recovers.

Dressed as Batman, Green Arrow goes off to battle villains. He can't get the hang of the Batarangs, so he uses his bow and arrows instead. Criminals keep attacking! Can he hold them off? In Gotham Harbor, Aquaman works hard to stop a robbery by the Penguin and his henchman.

"How does Batman do this alone?" Green Arrow and Aquaman wonder.

Shazam sees a group of criminals trying to steal a gold statue. Can Shazam stop them?

Like his friends, he asks, "How does Batman do this alone?"

Plastic Man confronts Catwoman at the Gotham City Zoo. He tricks her into a cage. "I'm really more of a dog person," he jokes.

An explosion rocks Gotham City and the four heroes rush to investigate. They meet up in a park.

"I'm Batman," insists Green Arrow.

"Outrageous!" argues Aquaman. "I'm Batman."

The pretend Caped Crusaders bicker about who the real Batman is . . . until . . . ZAP! The Joker knocks them out with a powerful blast from his stun gun!

Batman must locate his friends and help them! Still injured, he sets out to find them. Meanwhile, the Joker brags about his evil plan to the captive heroes.

"Once I gas Gotham City," crows the Joker, "I'm going global!" A giant jack-in-the-box pops open and a clown head springs up. The huge box cruises above the city, spraying laughing gas.

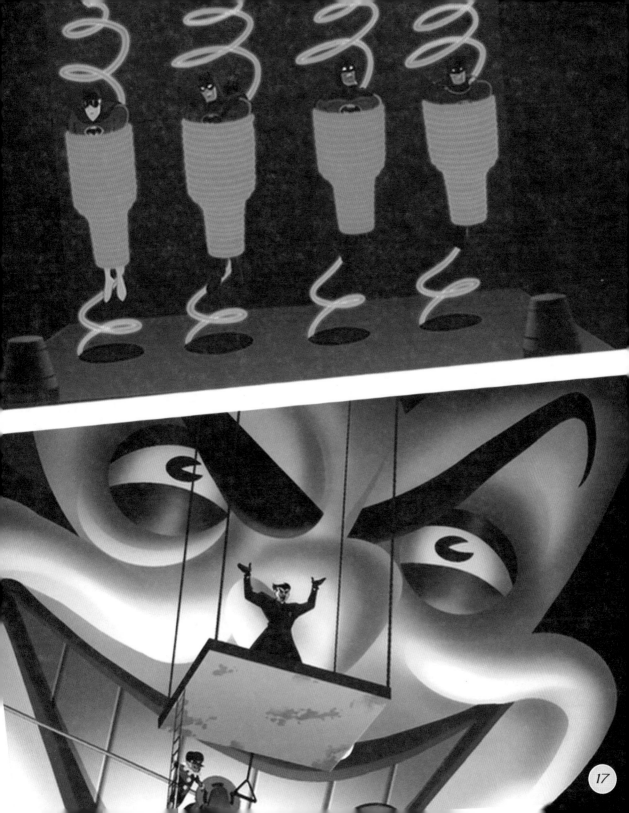

Batman's friends manage to escape and head off to battle the Joker's henchmen. Will they be able to help in time? But wait! The real Batman arrives to save the day and send the Joker back to Arkham Asylum.

"Ha, ha, ha! You're out of time," the Joker laughs.

"There's always time for justice," replies Batman. He hurls a Batarang at the jack-in-the-box's controls—and crashes the ship.

Working together, Batman and his friends defeat the Joker and his henchmen.

"Thank you for protecting Gotham City," Batman tells the other heroes. "But remember—there is only one Batman!" ZOOM! In front of him, a wormhole opens. More heroes dressed as Batman step out!

zzZOOMM

"We heard you need some help," says a copycat
Caped Crusader.
Batman sighs . . . and smiles.
"Just for tonight," he agrees. "Let's go!"
Ready to defend Gotham City from any criminals,
the heroes team up with Batman!